Food
PASTA

Louise Spilsbury

Heinemann Library
Chicago, Illinois

© 2001 Reed Educational & Professional Publishing
Published by Heinemann Library,
an imprint of Reed Educational & Professional Publishing,
Chicago, IL

Customer Service 888-454-2279

Visit our website at www.heinemannlibrary.com

Designed by Celia Floyd
Illustrated by Barry Atkinson
Originated by Ambassador Litho
Printed by South China Printing Co. in Hong Kong

05 04 03 02 01
10 9 8 7 6 5 4 3 2 1

Library of Congress Cataloging-in-Publication Data
Spilsbury, Louise.
  Pasta / Louise Spilsbury.
    p. cm. -- (Food)
Includes bibliographical references and index.
  ISBN 1-58810-148-7 (library binding)
  1. Pasta products--Juvenile literature. 2. Cookery (Pasta)--Juvenile
literature. [1. Pasta products.] I. Title. II. Series.
  TX394.5 .S65 2001
  641.8'22--dc21

                                00-012520

Acknowledgments
The Publishers would like to thank the following for permission to reproduce photographs:
AKG, p. 8; Anthony Blake Photo Library, pp. 10, 16; Gareth Boden, pp. 5, 6, 7, 22, 23, 28, 29; Dr. Eckart Pott/Bruce Coleman Collection, p. 12; Corbis, pp. 17, 20; Philip de Bay/Corbis, p. 9; Owen Franken/Corbis, p.18; John Heseltine/Corbis, p. 14; Vittoriano Rastelli/Corbis, pp. 15, 19, 21; Robert Harding, p. 4; Tony Stone Images, pp. 11, 24, 25.

Cover photograph reproduced with permission of Gareth Boden.

Some words are shown in bold, **like this.** You can find out what they mean by looking in the glossary.

Contents

What Is Pasta?

Pasta is an important food for many people across the world. In Italy, most people eat pasta every day.

Pasta is made from **flour** and water. These are its main **ingredients.** They are mixed to a paste, sometimes with egg or oil. The word *pasta* means "paste" in Italian.

Kinds of Pasta

Pasta can be made with **wheat** or white **flour.** Other foods, like tomato or spinach, may be added to give a different color and flavor.

white

wheat

tomato

spinach

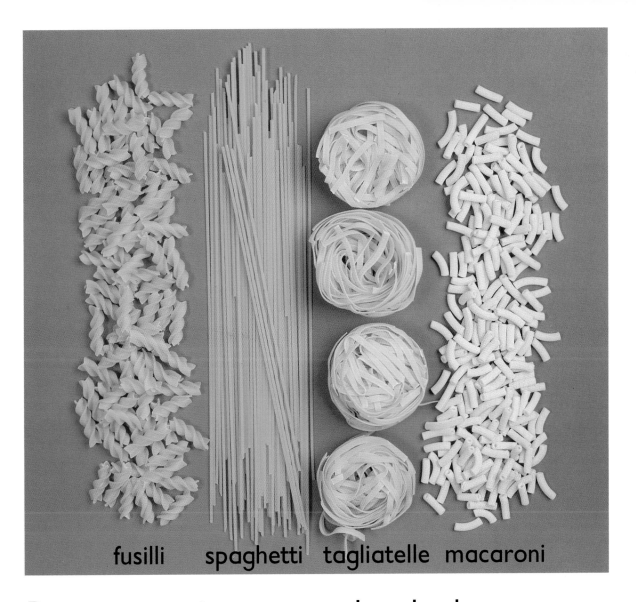

fusilli   spaghetti tagliatelle macaroni

Pasta comes in over one hundred shapes and sizes. Different kinds of pasta all have their own names. These names are usually Italian.

7

In the Past

There is a story that the Italian traveler Marco Polo brought the first pasta from China to Italy about 700 years ago. If so, he may have traveled in a ship like one of these.

Many people say that pasta was eaten in Italy before this time. Poor people ate a lot of pasta because it was cheap.

Around the World

Today pasta is eaten all over the world. In many countries, spaghetti is one of the most popular kinds of pasta.

In Asia, many people eat noodles. The noodles are made from **wheat** or other kinds of **flour.** They are a little like spaghetti.

Looking at Wheat

Pasta **flour** is made from **grains** of **wheat.** A machine crushes the grains into a powder. The grains grow at the top of the **stalk** on a wheat plant.

grains

stalk

leaf

White flour is made from the
endosperm of the wheat grain.
Wheat flour is brown. It is made
using the layer of **bran** as well.

A wheat
grain

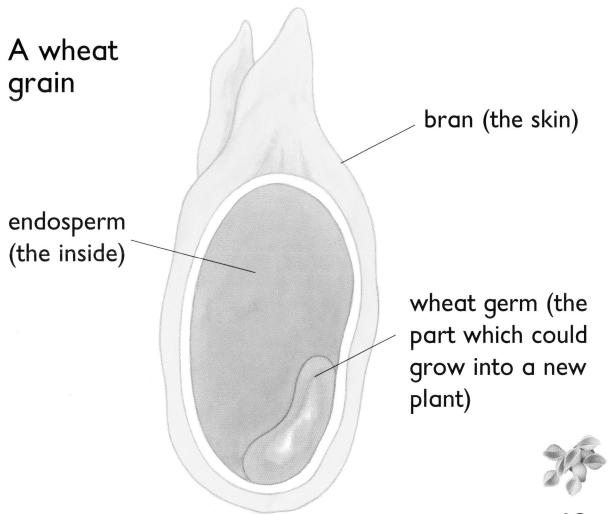

bran (the skin)

endosperm
(the inside)

wheat germ (the
part which could
grow into a new
plant)

13

Fresh and Dried

Some people make fresh pasta at home. They mix **flour,** water, and egg into a thick **dough.** They push it through a machine to make pasta shapes. You can also buy fresh pasta in shops.

Most people use **dried** pasta, which is made in **factories.** You can keep it for a long time before you cook it. Freshly made pasta does not keep for long.

Making Pasta

Dried pasta is made by machines. Computers tell them what to do. First the machines measure out the correct amounts of **flour** and water.

The flour and water are put into large tubs. Machines mix and **knead** them together to make a thick **dough.**

Cutting and Shaping

When the **dough** is ready, it goes into a pressing machine. This machine presses the dough through metal plates with holes in them.

To make spaghetti, the holes are round and very small. The shape and size of the holes are what make the different kinds of pasta.

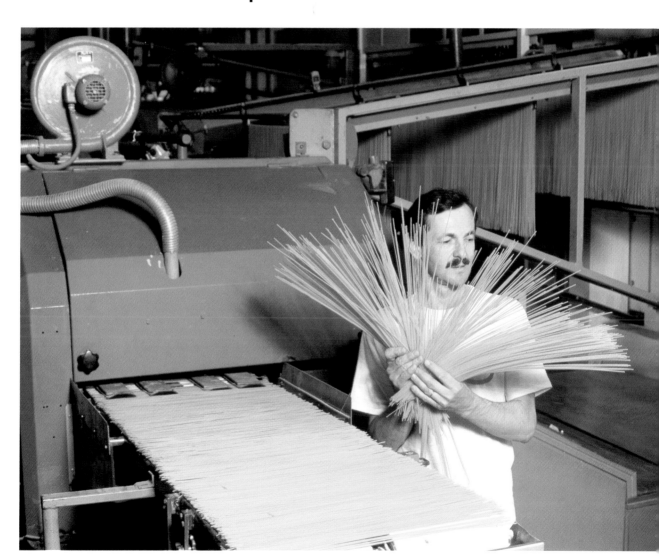

Drying and Packing

The pasta is **dried** using blasts of hot air. Then it is checked and measured so it is ready to be packed.

Finally, a machine weighs the dried pasta and drops it into packages. Labels tell **consumers** all about the pasta inside.

Eating Pasta

People don't usually eat pasta by itself. It is cooked for five to twelve minutes in boiling water. Then a vegetable, cheese, or meat sauce is poured over the top.

Some pasta is shaped to hold fillings inside. **Ravioli** are little pasta packages stuffed with meat or cheese. **Cannelloni** are pasta tubes baked with fillings inside.

ravioli   cannelloni

Good for You

Pasta is a **carbohydrate.** This means it is a kind of food that gives you **energy.** You use up energy in everything you do.

People who exercise a lot often eat pasta. The energy that pasta gives them lasts a long time. Pasta gives runners **stamina.**

Healthy Eating

The food guide **pyramid** shows how much of each different kind of food you should eat every day.

All of the food groups are important, but your body needs more of some foods than others.

You should eat more of the foods at the bottom and the middle of the pyramid. You should eat less of the foods at the top.

Pasta is in the **grain** group. Your body needs six servings of foods in the grain group each day.

Fats and Sweets
Eat less

Milk Group
2 servings

Meat Group
2 servings

Vegetable
Group
servings

Fruit Group
2 servings

Grain Group   6 servings

Based on the Food Guide Pyramid for Young Children, U.S. Department of
Agriculture, Center for Nutrition Policy and Promotions, March 1999.

Pasta Salad Recipe

1. To cook the pasta, put it into a pot of boiling water. Boil it for about 12 minutes (check time needed on the package).

2. Use a **colander** to drain the pasta. Leave it in a bowl until it is cold.

You will need:
- 1 cup (225 grams) pasta
- water
- 3/4 cup (175 grams) cheese
- 1 red pepper
- half a cucumber
- salad dressing

colander ——

Ask an adult to help you!

3. Cut the cheese, red pepper, and cucumber into small pieces. Add these to the pasta.

4. Stir in a large spoonful of salad dressing to taste and serve.

Glossary

bran brown skin that covers a wheat grain

cannelloni tube made of pasta, filled with meat, cheese, or vegetables (You say can-el-OH-nee.)

carbohydrate part of food that the body uses to get energy

colander metal or plastic bowl with holes in it

consumer person who buys things that he or she needs or wants, like food

dough soft, thick mixture made with flour and water

dried to have all the water removed before packing

endosperm the inside of a grain of wheat

energy to be able and strong enough to do things

factory very large building where people and machines make things or food

fat part of some foods that the body uses to get energy and to keep warm

flour powder made by grinding the grains of some plants

grain   seed of a cereal plant

ingredient   food such as flour and oil, mixed or cooked together to make another food, like pasta

knead   pulling and squeezing dough

pyramid   shape with a flat bottom and three sides with edges that come to a point

ravioli   package made of pasta, filled with meat, cheese, or vegetables (You say ra-vee-OH-lee.)

stalk   part of a plant that holds the leaves and flowers up above the ground

stamina   the energy to keep going for a long time, such as in a race or a long swim

wheat   type of plant with seeds that can be eaten

More Books to Read

Berger, Melvin. *Pasta Please!* New York: Newbridge Educational Publishing, 1996.

Corey, Melinda. *Let's Visit a Spaghetti Factory.* Mahway, N.J.: Troll Communications, 1990.

Julius, Jennifer. *I Like Pasta.* Danbury, Conn.: Children's Press, 2000.

Index